HIS Christmas STAR

About the Author

Elizabeth Lee Sorrell is an Alabama native. A gifted teacher, she has worked with babies and preschoolers, from her teens all the way to today. She is a teacher in the Federal Head Start program. She has her Associate's Degree in Early Childhood Development, her Bachelor's in Early Childhood Education and Elementary Education, and her Master's in Early Childhood Education.

When not teaching, or leading as the Nursery Coordinator of her church, she is with her family and dear friends, probably reading or writing a book. She loves to spend time with her nieces. Elizabeth is a Christian. She cheers for the Auburn Tigers, and the Atlanta Braves. As a big baseball fan, she has, more than once, written stories in the world of MLB, and watches as many games as she is able.

She enjoys pairing up with Sandra JS Coleman for her covers and illustrations. Sandra, Elizabeth's sister, is a graphic designer and an illustrator.

Learn more at www.ElizabethLeeSorrell.com

HIS Christmas STAR

Elizabeth Lee Sorrell

Yarbrough House Publishing, Inc.

Trading as Yabrough House Publishing, Inc.
For information please email
info@yarbroughhousepublishing.com

www.YarbroughHousePublishing.com

ISBN-978-0-9995800-7-3

First Edition.

Printed in the United States of America

Acknowledgements

I'd like to thank my family who really do all the hard work. While I sit back and make up fanciful stories, my family stays busy proofing, formatting, illustrating, crunching numbers, and taking care of all the "business stuff." All I do is play with my imagination, but my family works hard to bring life to my stories.

Chapter One

Star Clause was a name that Declan could not get
out of his head. More than that, he couldn't get the girl
herself out of his head. He didn't want to either. Star
was a dazzling character who was... unforgettable. She
had ivory skin that was smooth and flawless everywhere
you could see. Her hair was as black as night but with a
radiant shine. She looked like an angel but dressed like
temptation. She moved with grace when she fought. She
fought like a girl, yet she didn't hold back. Everything she
did was with a flare that was totally Star.

Declan never denied being a ladies' man. He knew
the whole town talked. Their tongues must have really
been wagging lately, because Declan had not been on a
date in over eight months. He hadn't been interested in

other girls since he met Star. She was out of his league, but he couldn't help himself. They'd been writing each other since they parted ways in March. It was late November now, and he couldn't wait to see her again.

He rushed home from work after a peewee hockey practice to find a letter from Star waiting on him.

Dear Declan,

I'm so bored! I can't stand another hotel room. I think if your offer to show me the South Pole is still good, I'm ready to take you up on it. Would right away be a good time?

I have exciting news! Israel's oldest daughter is pregnant! It's so exciting when my nieces start having kids. I miss Noel like crazy. I'm sure I'll love this one just as much. We haven't heard what she's having yet. Don't tell the others, but I really hope she has a girl. This child will be close to Noel's age, and when Noel takes her place fighting vampires, it helps having someone who isn't new to the world outside of the North Pole.

I remember when I first turned eighteen. The world was a scary place. It is so different from the North Pole, and I had never known anything else. We were all trained by aunts or uncles, but I had an aunt who took me under her wing. She helped me acclimate to my new world. I would have been lost without her. We lost her just before Mary's eighteenth birthday.

I honestly don't think Mary had anyone past training. Perhaps that was why life was difficult for her. I do wish she could find happiness again.

Girls are more fun to shop for too! I've bought Noel a mess of clothes for Christmas! I imagine between her dad and grandfather she'll get more toys than she'll ever need. Someone has to keep the girl dressed.

Write me back soon. I do so want to see the South Pole and you.

Love,

Star

Declan wasted no time. He scribbled out a note right then.

Dear Star,

Right now would be perfect. I want to see you too.

Love,

Declan

Another week passed, and Declan didn't hear anything else from Star until the first of December when there was an uproar in the middle of town.

"What is she doing here?" a voice grumbled.

"I thought they agreed to peace. Why would one of them be here?"

Peace? Them? It must have been one of the Clauses. Maybe they had word from Star or at least knew why he hadn't heard back from her. Declan pushed his way to the front of the crowd, and his breath caught when he saw a vision dressed in hot pink snow gear.

"But, I'm looking for someone. They're expecting me," she said.

"Star!" Declan called out.

"See!" Star pouted in victory then ran to meet Declan.

He immediately pulled her into a bear hug. "How did you get here?"

"I used magic, silly. There was no direct flight to the South Pole, but I think I caused a ruckus."

"Who cares? You're here."

"Yeah, I just got your letter. You said now was perfect, so here I am."

"How long are you staying?"

"I'm not sure."

"Where are you staying?"

"I'm not sure of that either. Are there hotels down here?"

"Sure, let's go get you checked in."

"Good, I brought some things," Star said with a wave of her hand and two large suitcases appeared at her side.

Declan laughed then with one hand he grabbed the bigger suitcase and the other arm he wrapped around her waist. As he walked he planned. He was torn whether to put her in the nicest hotel or the one closest to his place. There were only three to choose from in all of the South Pole.

"What is more important to you?" he asked. "The amenities or the locale?"

"I want the authentic experience," she answered with a gratifying grin.

"I wish I could put you up in my parents' spare room," Declan mused.

"Why don't you?"

"Ah… they'd just as soon shoot you as look at you."

"Oh, that's too bad. I'd like to say my parents would have behaved differently, but it would be a lie. I won't be meeting your parents then?"

"I don't know. I want for you to, but I'd better talk to them before we show up on their doorstep."

"You're probably right. Clause magic can do a lot of things, but dead is dead."

Declan knew that Star had meant that as a joke, but he didn't find anything funny about her death.

"So, what sorts of things can your magic do?"

"I can spruce up any hotel room, so let's find the most convenient."

"There's one less than two miles from my house, but it leaves a lot to be desired. I'm afraid I don't live on the nicest side of town."

"That one would be perfect. Will you show me your house too?"

"Of course, I'll show you anything you want to see."

"I want to see everything. This is what I've always wanted. I've dreamed of coming to the South Pole since I was a little girl."

"I hope you're not disappointed."

"Look at this place!" Star said pulling Declan in a complete circle. "It's perfect!"

"Yeah?" Declan chuckled. "What's so perfect?"

"It's everything I had growing up and everything I didn't. I loved the North Pole. Its clear skies, uncluttered, unpolluted. The clean, crisp smell of snow." She took a deep breath that caused her whole body to heave. "The scenic beauty is all around, but here you're not alone. You have friends. You have other people to interact with. The only people I had growing up were my parents and siblings."

"Yeah, I guess so. How many years ago did you leave the North Pole shouldn't you be used to people by now?"

"You would think so… It's not over populated here like the rest of the world either."

Declan was sorry to see when they got to the hotel that it was more dilapidated than he had remembered. "I'm sorry, Star. I can't ask you to stay here."

"Do you know where Wynter stayed when she was down here?"

"No, Noah's always been a bit vague on that point."

"She stayed in a cave."

"No way! You've got to be kidding me. She really did that. Noah's mentioned a cave, but I never thought he was serious. How could she have survived the weather?"

Star waved her fingers in front of Declan's face and said, "I can make any place habitable. Come on." Then she pulled him inside the hotel lobby.

The door creaked terribly as they pulled it open. It needed more than a little oil; it needed a lot of work. It was nothing a screwdriver and a little elbow grease couldn't solve, but it didn't need work as much as the rest of the building.

"I need one room, please," Star smiled sweetly at the clerk.

He was eyeing the blindingly pink snow suit Star sported without so much as cracking a smile. He didn't come across as overly friendly, but at least he wasn't hostile. When his dark eyes finally moved to Star's face he barked, "Name?"

"Star Clause."

"Is this some kind of joke?" Now the man was addressing Declan. "We don't take Clauses at this establishment. We have standards. I don't take kindly to obnoxious jokes either. Both of you get out of here. I don't want to see you back in here again. You're not welcome. I'll call the police if you show your faces here again trying to cause trouble."

"Cause trouble? Look no one wants any trouble. The lady just wants a room. Isn't her money just as good as anyone else's? It certainly looks like you could use the money around here," Declan returned heatedly.

"That's ok, Declan. I understand. We'll try another one of the hotels."

Star wrapped her arm around Declan's and pulled him toward the door. He caught her waving her fingers in front of her just as the door tightened on its hinges.

Declan pulled the door open and found it surprisingly silent, it moved smoothly.

"What did you do?" Declan demanded as he turned back to look at the door over his shoulder. Much to his surprise, the whole hotel had gotten a much needed face lift. There was no doubt Star was to thank. "What did you do that for?"

"It needed it."

"So? That guy was awful to you just now. He won't appreciate what you did for him."

"I didn't do it to be appreciated. I did it because he needed a helping hand."

"What is with you Clauses? Do you have some kind of do good gene or something?"

"We have the same genes you do, silly. You would have done the same thing."

"No, I definitely would not have helped that creep out. He needs to be knocked out."

"I helped out a stranger who had never shown me a bit of kindness. You traveled all the way to the North Pole to help out an entire family of strangers who had never shown you a bit of kindness. You would do the same thing."

"I did that because it was the right thing to do."

"So was this. Now, where is the next hotel?"
There was finality to her tone, and Declan knew the
conversation was over. He knew before today that she was
hot as sin with a quirky personality that made him smile,
yet he never dreamed her heart was that large.

He wished the same could be said of his own people.
The clerk from the first hotel must have already called
ahead to warn the other hotels. There were signs on the
front door of both hotels that said in big bold letters
NO CLAUSES ALLOWED.

Now what? Noah and Lorelei had room, but he
hated to impose on the newlyweds. They had gotten
married not long after they all returned from the North
Pole. Lorelei's nightmare of a roommate was evicting
her. Lorelei couldn't afford another place, so she and
Noah used it as an excuse to get married right away and
moved her into his place.

Declan's parents had the room, but they wouldn't
treat her much better. Star had been in the South Pole
all of an hour, and so far she had encountered hate and
bigotry every step of her journey. At this rate, she'd
leave again in no time. Declan didn't want to see her go
so soon. On the other hand he wanted to tuck her away

somewhere and shield her from all the hate. He could always give her his bed, and he'd sleep on the couch.

"Well, we could always give Noah a call to show us to Wynter's cave. I'm sure she wouldn't mind me staying at her place," Star said optimistically.

"Absolutely not. I'm not letting you live in a cave like some caveman while you're here. We'll call my parents."

"I don't want to be any trouble."

"Nah, they have plenty of space." That was true. He left out the part that they hated her already. There was no sense pointing out the obvious.

Chapter Two

Declan called ahead to tell his parents he was coming over with a friend who needed a place to stay, but he didn't go into any detail about who the friend was or where she came from.

Star was surprised to see Mr. and Mrs. Anderson greet her and Declan at the door. They were both wearing huge, priceless smiles, and Mrs. Anderson looked absolutely beside herself to see them. Did Declan not ever visit his own parents?

"Come on inside. Let's get out of the cold," Mrs. Anderson insisted. "I don't think Declan has ever brought a girl home before. You are so beautiful, and I love that outfit. Where in the world did you find a snowsuit that pink?"

"Oh, thank you. I do love to shop," Star replied.

"How did you and Declan meet?"

"I wanted to talk to you about that actually," Declan interrupted. "Maybe we should all go sit down first."

"Sure, we've got the guest room all set up for you. I put fresh sheets on the bed. It has been so long since anyone slept in there."

"Thank you, but you really didn't have to go to any trouble," Star admitted.

"Don't be silly. I was starting to think that Declan would never settle down. I mean I had hoped that after Noah got married and settled down that Declan would follow his lead. I've worried about those boys and Kyson too. Kyson and Vivienne are sort of on again off again. We don't ever know what's going on with those two, but my Declan he's never had a real steady girl."

"Mom," Declan said and cleared his throat.

"Well, I'm your mother. It's my job to worry about these things. What's your name, dear?"

"I'm Star."

"We really need to talk," Declan interrupted before Star could give her last name.

She stuck her hand out anyway. She wasn't going to be uncongenial. Star noticed instantly how soft Mrs.

Anderson's hand was. "What kind of lotion do you use? I remember growing up in the cold weather how hard it was to keep my skin from drying out."

"Oh, I make it myself. I'll get you some to try before you leave. I'll give the recipe to you also if you'd like."

"That would be lovely."

"So, you don't live around here anymore?" Mrs. Anderson questioned.

"No, I'm actually not from here at all."

"That's what I want to talk to you about, Mom. Please have a seat," Declan pushed.

They had made it to the living room. It was done in warm, neutral browns and whites. It was a cozy room with a large fireplace. Star could imagine a family curling up in front of the fire to share about their day with one another.

Mrs. Anderson sat down with an exasperated sigh and said, "What is it Declan?"

"Star, didn't grow up here or anywhere near here," Declan started. His eyes were darting back and forth between him mom and dad, who were sitting in matching recliners separated only by a small end table.

Star took a seat on the edge of the couch and waited for the other foot to fall. The couch was fluffy and much more comfortable than it looked. This was the kind of room her mother used to say drew a family together. You make your family room the most comfortable room in the house so that you're assured your family will gather together her mom would always tell her.

"What are you getting at, son?" Mr. Anderson asked. He had a deep voice. It was a voice that portrayed strength. It was the kind of voice that upon hearing it, you just knew you could depend on that kind of man.

"We met earlier this year, in the spring."

"Yes?" Mrs. Anderson nudged when it sounded like Declan wouldn't finish.

It really did sound like Declan wasn't going to finish. Even now he just looked back and forth at his parents waiting for them to guess a thing. "This is silly. Just tell them… I'm from the North Pole. My last name is Clause. I'm Star Clause, and I met Declan when he and his friends went to the North Pole back in March. He's scared to tell you, because he knows that you'll be upset."

"WHAT?" Mr. Anderson roared.

"Oh dear me!" Mrs. Anderson sobbed and clutched her chest like as though it might jump from her chest. And, to think Star's family called her a drama queen! Really?

"It's really not that bad," Star continued, but was cut off by Mr. Anderson.

"Get out of my house right now."

"Dad, she has nowhere else to go. None of the hotels would give her a room," Declan pleaded.

"And, neither will we."

"Where will she stay?"

"Let her go back where she came from."

"She came here to see me and to see the South Pole. I won't send her away... Mom, please; I've never asked you for anything like this before."

"That's true. He hasn't," Mrs. Anderson told Mr. Anderson.

"I won't have a Clause staying under my roof."

"Supposing he doesn't bring the next girl home to meet us?"

"Humph."

"Supposing there isn't another girl?" On that thought Mrs. Anderson's eyes widened and began to tear up. "Supposing he leaves home and never comes back? You said one child was good enough for anyone, Ralph Anderson. You said that. Now, you can't run my only child off. You can't do it!"

"Woman, I won't have a Clause in my house." His words were insistent, but his tone was softening.

Somewhere in the midst of all the arguing Declan had sidestepped between Star and his parents. He fumbled behind him reaching for Star, so she grabbed his hand with her own. His hand was warm, and he held her hand tight. It was reassuring in a way. This was his world after all, and Star didn't really know what to expect. She especially didn't want to cause a rift between him and his parents. Surely Declan wouldn't have brought her here if he didn't believe things could be reconciled.

"It's ok, Mom. She can stay with me. I'll sleep on the couch. We could always go vacation somewhere more neutral. It's just that Star has always wanted to see the South Pole. I wanted to give her the grand tour, show off the South Pole, you know. I wanted her to love it here as much as I do," Declan said in a pathetic voice that was as fake as a red nosed reindeer.

"Oh, Ralph, I don't ask you for much," Mrs. Anderson begged desperately although Star wasn't sure why. The woman had not so much as looked Star's way since finding out she was a Clause.

"You ask for a lot, woman." Mr. Anderson heaved a long suffering sigh. "But, I'd give you the world if I could."

"Oh, Ralph!" Mrs. Anderson squealed in delight. She bounded out of her recliner and bounced into Mr. Anderson's lap with a kiss to his cheek. It was all very cute, and Star hoped that she could find love and devotion like that one day.

"Come on," Declan whispered and pulled Star up from the couch. He pulled her up a set of stairs and down a hallway to the second door on the right. He tugged her into the darkened room and shut the door behind them. He spun her around until her back was against the wall. Then he reached over her shoulder and flipped a light switch on.

Before Star's eyes could adjust to the light, Declan leaned into her and kissed her. He tasted like the perfect blend of sweet and salty. She could taste sugar cookies.

Sugar cookies always reminded her of her dad. She had such fond memories of her dad; she was such a daddy's girl. Bacon, that was it! Bacon and sugar cookies, it was a combination that was all Star, or at least she thought it was. She had always loved the unconventional combination, and that was exactly what Declan tasted like.

"Is this what it's like?" Star asked a little breathlessly.

"What's that?" Declan whispered against her lips in a deliciously deep, sexy voice.

"Sneaking behind your parents' back. I never did that sort of thing. The only other boys in the North Pole were all my brothers."

Declan laughed. Oops, maybe she had said too much. Oh well, live with no regrets. With that mantra in mind, Star wrapped her arms around his neck and pulled Declan in for another kiss.

"Mmm, you taste like bacon and sugar cookies."

"That would be the bacon cheeseburger I had for lunch and a sugar cookie this afternoon."

"I like it. I eat bacon and sugar cookies together."

"That's... That's, uh... That's different." Declan kissed her again and said, "You taste like strawberries and mint."

"Toothpaste and lip gloss."

"I like it." That was what he said before he dove in for another taste.

They stayed right there tasting until a knock at the door interrupted their feast. "Declan?" Mrs. Anderson called from the other side of the door.

Declan stepped away from Star and opened the door. Star finally got her first good look at the room as he opened the door for his mother. The room was done in soft grays. Black and white family photos decorated the room. Star had never seen something so simple look so beautiful and elegant before. The duvet covering the bed looked so cushy that Star couldn't resist. She went right over and sat down as Mrs. Anderson moved into the room.

"Oh, Mrs. Anderson, this room is divine!"

"Yes... Are you staying for dinner?" The question was directed at Declan. Curious herself Star waited for his answer.

"Sure, Mom."

"Are you sure it isn't any trouble? I hate that we just dropped in like this, especially all things considered."

"It's fine." Mrs. Anderson was polite but quick and to the point. She was no longer excited to see that Declan had brought home a girl.

"Mom, I really think you'll like Star if you give her a chance."

Mrs. Anderson nodded but said nothing to that. She saw herself out making a point to push the door open wide on her way out. It was clear that she didn't think Declan and Star should be alone in there with the door shut.

This was a side of dating that Star had never experienced before. Was that what they were doing? Were they dating, or was this vacation only?

Chapter Three

Declan decided not to push his mom any further. She was being rather gracious under the circumstances. He left the door open, walked to the opposite side of the bed, and laid down next to Star. She immediately leaned back and stretched out next to him.

"So, you've never brought a girl home to meet your parents?"

"I guess not."

"I think I disappointed your mom."

"She'll get over it."

"I don't know. She seems pretty uncomfortable with me."

"What about you?"

"What about me?"

"Are you comfortable staying here? I meant what I said. You can have my bed, and I'll take the couch." Declan wanted to make Star as comfortable as he could while she was here.

"Don't be silly. I'm already here. See, look," she said and pointed to a corner of the room where her bags suddenly appeared.

"Now I feel stupid for loading them in the car the old fashioned way," Declan laughed.

Star smiled and said, "Tell me about the South Pole's history."

"I don't know that much to tell. History wasn't really my thing in school."

"What was your thing?"

"Sports and girls in that order."

"Ah, I see… Don't you find it fascinating that the North and South Poles are the only two places you find magic outside of the demonic realm?"

"I haven't really thought about it that much," Declan admitted. He wasn't an intellectual. He hadn't thought until now that Star went for the brainy kind.

"I just think it has to be more than a coincidence. The job of Santa is passed down from father to son, and the others hunt vampires. It has been that way for generations, and given the natural length of our life spans, you're talking about a long time… I guess it's hard to keep up with much before that, if there ever was anything before that. I know that Clause history is kept in the attic of the family home. That's where Santa lives. Mother never wanted us playing up there, because it was so dirty. At that age, I tended to agree with her, but I wish I had an idea now what all is up there."

"Why don't you go see?"

"I don't know. I stay pretty busy most of the time."

"Take some time off. Visit your family. Christmas is coming. Do it for yourself as a Christmas present."

Star didn't say anything. She was staring up at the ceiling lost in thought. Declan reached over and took her hand in his. He wasn't sure why he did it. He just wanted to touch her. "What do you think will be up there?"

Star turned her head to look Declan in the eyes. "Promise not to laugh?" she asked in a serious tone.

"Promise." He gave her hand a reassuring squeeze.

"I have a theory that the South Pole and the North Pole must have some sort of connection, something before the feud. I want to find what came before the feud, what started the feud."

"You're obsessed with this feud, aren't you?"

"No, not really. I'm obsessed with anything and everything South Pole. I always have been. My grandfather called it an unhealthy obsession. Mother would always pat his hand and tell him it was natural curiosity of the unknown and that a little was healthy. If she hadn't been curious when my dad told her he was Santa, she never would have followed him to the North Pole."

"Healthy or not, I'm glad you're curious."

"I just bet you are, lady killer."

"Lady killer?"

"I'm beginning to figure you out, Declan Anderson."

"That's too bad. I was trying so hard to impress you."

He rolled over and started to lean in for a kiss when his dad bellowed from the doorway, "DECLAN! Come downstairs. Food's ready."

¤ ¤ ¤ ¤ ¤

Mr. Anderson was burley and sour throughout dinner. Thankfully Declan didn't get his personality from his dad; he did get his appearance from his dad though. Mr. Anderson was tall, medium build. He was made of lean compacted muscles. His medium build disguised his athletic tone. He had dark hair and eyes, and although the dark eyes on Mr. Anderson looked moody, on Declan they were mysterious and offered endless depths. They didn't have a very dark tan for most worldly standards, but for the extreme poles, they were absolutely tropical. If you looked close enough there was a hint of barely there dimples. Perfectly straight, perfectly white teeth sat tucked behind full lips and a strong jaw.

"This is delicious, Mrs. Anderson," Star said trying to prompt conversation.

"Thank you."

"Mom loves to cook," Declan offered.

"I've never been any good. Heaven knows I tried. I wanted so badly to be a good cook. I finally had to accept defeat and admit that I was much better at ordering out," Star told.

No one said anything.

"Maybe you could teach Star to cook a few things?" Declan urged his mom.

She only froze in place and looked at him.

"I'm afraid I'm hopeless. It turned out I was better at fighting than domesticating." At that admission, Mr. Anderson began choking on his water. "I have a flare for fashion and decorating," Star added.

"Star does everything with a flare. You should see her fighting style sometime. I've never seen anyone who fights with sparkle and glitter before."

Mrs. Anderson's face turned pale. Her eyes widened and she stared at Declan and Star as if they had both grown horns and stood to dance naked on the table.

"I don't think there are any vampires around here. There aren't too many like Anthony running around," Star tried to back pedal.

"Anthony Phillips? He was a lovely young man. How do you know him?" Mrs. Anderson sounded highly defensive. Well, at least that was one thing she had going for her. She liked Anthony.

"You know my nephew!"

"Anthony Phillips was not a Clause!" Mrs. Anderson sputtered.

"Was being the key word. He wasn't a Clause until he married my niece, and viola, a Clause was born."

"I-I think I'm done," Mrs. Anderson whispered before rushing from the room.

Star looked to Declan with guilt weighing her down. "I'm sorry. I just… I'm sorry."

"It's not your fault," he assured her and leaned in to kiss her temple.

That wasn't true. It was her fault. All she had wanted was to find a common ground. That was the last thing anyone around here wanted. Maybe North had been right. He had warned her no good would come from going to the South Pole. It wasn't that he necessarily had anything against the South Pole people. She was pretty sure that North would adopt Lorelei as his own if given the chance, but a prejudice older than anyone can remember wouldn't be cured over night.

"I should go," Star said placing her napkin on the table. It was best she leave before she did anymore damage.

"No!" Declan stood from his chair and placed a firm hand on Star's shoulder to hold her in hers. "I haven't even shown you around yet."

"I know. I regret not getting to see more, but it's probably best if I go."

"I don't want you to go."

"She's right, Declan. Let her go," Mr. Anderson seconded.

"Would you just stay out of this? Haven't you and Mom done enough damage?" Declan snapped at his dad.

"I will not be talked to that way in my own house!" Mr. Anderson's face was as red as Santa's suit.

"Good, it was a mistake to come here in the first place!" Declan grabbed Star's hand and tugged her from her chair and intended to leave the house. Star stood but held her ground.

"Declan, please."

"You want to stay here?" he asked indignantly.

"I don't want to be the cause of a family quarrel."

Declan placed a gentle hand on Star's cheek. "It's not you. You're so receptive, ready for a change. They're the ones being pigheaded."

"Change is hard. They won't be the only ones. You can't fight everyone for me."

"I can try."

"That's sweet, but no." A single thought and Star had luggage in hand. A second thought and she was back in America in the latest hotel she called home. She had been a fool to believe she could visit the South Pole, but now it was worse somehow. She was giving up more than just a lifelong dream of seeing the South Pole. She was leaving Declan behind. He was just another in a long line of acquaintances that had come and gone in her life. Star collapsed onto the bed and cried herself to sleep.

Chapter Four

The next morning Star couldn't find the will power
to pull herself out of bed, but she had three older
brothers. That's what family was for, to pick you up when
you were down.

Somehow Star was able to wiggle her phone free
from her pocket and dial North.

"Hello?" His voice was gruff like he had been
asleep. Star had no idea what time it was. He might have
been asleep.

"North, I need you."

"Did they hurt you?" he asked urgently. His voice
wasn't sleep roughened any longer.

"No... yes... I don't know. I don't want to get out of
bed... ever again."

"Where are you?"

"I'm at the Sunset Marquis."

"In Hollywood? What are you doing there?"

"The way Hollywood has glamorized vampires, they can hide in plain sight around here."

"Stay put. I'm on my way."

Star let her head fall back to the bed, and she waited. It took North longer than she had expected. That was when she realized that she hadn't given him her room number. Never mind, he'd find her. He always found her.

North had been the first of her older brothers to leave the North Pole, and Star had been terrified. She had been so young when North left home, only six years old. She was sure that he was going to get lost without the reindeer to guide him, and she'd never see him again. The night before he left, he sat Star down in his lap and made her a promise.

"I will always find you. No matter where I go, no matter where you go, I will always find you," he had said.

And, he had always found her. He had never broken his promise. When their parents died and Star thought her world would end, North found her. He had this sort of sixth sense that Star couldn't identify.

"Star?"

Star rolled over so that she could see North. Judging by his reaction, she must have looked worse than she thought.

"Oh, baby, what happened? Come here," and just like that North was pulling her into his lap like she was still that six year old girl.

"You were right. I shouldn't have gone. They have three hotels that apparently all three have a no Clause clause. Not that it surprised me. Declan took me to stay with his parents. I told him I could just stay in Wynter's cave, but he didn't want that. His parents hated me, and I was causing a fight between him and his parents. Family is important. I can't come between him and his parents, so I left."

"Yeah?"

"Yeah."

"And, now you don't want to get out of bed? You want to stay in bed and cry?"

"I didn't want to leave, and I'm not crying."

"Then what is this rolling down your cheeks?" North asked wiping wet from her face.

"I'm crying," Star sounded surprised. She was surprised. She thought she had cried herself out last night. She hadn't even noticed the tears this morning.

"Star, why are you crying?" He was using his big brother voice, the one that meant you'd better answer him or else. It was a really parent thing to do, even if he wasn't her dad.

"I miss Declan."

"Already?"

"I started missing him the second I knew I had to leave."

"Then what are you doing here?"

"What do you mean?"

"Why aren't you with Declan?"

"I told you. I can't be with Declan."

"I see. Well, you can't fight like this. Come on. Get up. Get your stuff."

"Where are we going?"

"You are going to the North Pole for a little R & R." What he wasn't saying was that he was confining Star to the North Pole until she got her head screwed on straight, but Santa would keep a close eye on her.

¤ ¤ ¤ ¤ ¤

It had been a week since Declan stormed out of his parents' house. He hadn't talked to them, wasn't taking their phone calls. It was childish. It was, but he hadn't heard a single word from Star in that week either. There hadn't been any letters from her. He had written her plenty, but he didn't know if they were finding their way to her.

It was like he had lost something... something important. He felt it all the way to his core, or rather he didn't feel it. He felt hallow inside. Declan had never had a steady girlfriend, but he imagined that's what this felt like. Star had only been in the South Pole for a matter of hours, yet already it wasn't the same without her. It no longer felt like home.

He was being stupid. Logically he knew that. They barely knew each other. They had spent less than two days together, yet... this didn't feel like anything he had ever felt before. There had been countless other women

in Declan's life, but this thing with Star was different. He certainly hadn't been empty before Star. It was like she had carved out a place for herself inside him, and now she was gone leaving that carved out notch... bare. It could have been nothing more than Clause magic, but Declan didn't care. He had liked it, and he wanted it back.

All the emotional turmoil was taking its toll on work as well. Declan couldn't keep his head in the game, much less identify areas where his players needed extra work. He was packing up after a practice he didn't really remember, when Noah approached him.

"What have you done to upset North Clause?" Noah asked.

"Nothing I haven't seen or heard from him since March."

"Well, he's at the house right now with Lorelei, and he's not happy to be here."

"Then what's he doing here."

"He said he's looking for you. He seems pretty upset, and I didn't know if I should tell you to come over or run the other way."

"Listen, I-I'm right behind you," Declan sighed wondering what was up now.

"Not me. I've got an injured seal I need to check in on before I head home, but I'll meet you there. Be careful."

"Sure."

North and Lorelei were at the front door before Declan could get out of the car. "What did you do to my little sister, kid?" North demanded.

"Star? You've talked to her?"

"Yeah, I talked to her, and-"

"Is she ok?" Declan interrupted though North clearly wasn't finished speaking.

"No, she's not ok. What did you do?"

"Where is she?"

"North Pole. The only thing stopping me from hurting you right now is knowing that it would hurt her."

"Can I see her?"

North studied Declan for a moment before turning to Lorelei. "It was good to see you again. You take care, and thank Noah for tracking this kid down for me." Then he turned back to Declan and asked, "You ready?"

Before Declan could ask what for, he found himself no longer in front of Noah's house. A quick survey of his surrounding told Declan he was in the North Pole. Specifically he was in Santa's living room.

"Where is she?" he asked. The desperation in his voice made him sick, but there was no help for it.

"Most days she doesn't get out of bed."

"Star doesn't?"

"No, the Easter bunny, who do you think we're talking about?"

"Where is everyone else?"

"Out by the stables I think. Focus kid. Upstairs second door on the right. If you hurt her, I'll break your arms."

Although he didn't doubt the sincerity, Declan didn't care about North's threat. All he cared about was getting to Star, and he was half way up the stairs before North finished his threat.

The door was open, and Star was lying in the bed with the covers pulled up to her chin. Her dark hair was a tangled mess across the pillow case. "Star?"

A heart wrenching sob escaped Star, and Declan was crouched next to the bed in a second flat. He pushed wet, matted hair away from her face and gently asked, "What's wrong, Star?"

"You're really here!" she exclaimed.

She popped out of bed and wrapped herself around Declan causing him to fall flat on his butt. It didn't matter. Nothing mattered. Star was back in his arms, and he wasn't letting her go this time. He wrapped his long arms tightly around her tiny body.

"Where did you go?" he asked her.

"I went home… well the closest thing I had to home."

"Why did you leave me?"

"I can't come between you and your parents. Family is too important."

"You're too important. Star?"

"Mmm."

"Star, look at me." She pulled back just enough to look Declan in the face. "Please, don't ever leave like that again. I've been miserable without you."

"I was miserable too," Star admitted.

Then because he couldn't resist another second, he pressed his lips to hers. There was no strawberry lip gloss this time, but she was still the best thing he had ever tasted.

"Come back with me? I still want to show you the South Pole, where I grew up… You can stay in Wynter's cave this time if that's what you want."

"Can we look up South Pole records too?"

"Sure, if that's what you want."

"Only for a week. Then I'd like to come back here and show you where I grew up if that's ok?"

"I'd like that. A week in the South and a week in the North?" Declan proposed.

"Yeah, I like that."

Chapter Five

Star's magic put them right at the mouth of a cave. .
It was literally a cave, not even a very large one. Declan
could see inside the cave, and all he saw was rock and
shadows. There was no way anyone lived here.

"Must be the wrong one," Declan said.

"Nope, this is the place."

"Star, there's no way Roscoe fit in this cave, much
less Wynter and Roscoe together."

"Nothing is ever as it seems when magic is involved.
Watch and learn, Declan Anderson." Star took his hand
and drug him into the cave.

Once they passed the entrance, everything changed.
The first thing Declan noticed was the temperature.
There was actual heat inside the... cave. There was also

lighting, good lighting. What should have been bathed in darkness was bright and easily discernible. There was a full sized bed, a sitting area, and a full kitchenette all with a very open floor plan. It was neat and cozy. It wasn't real big, but it was as large as a nice sized hotel room which was what Star was used to after all.

"Is this going to be alright?" Declan asked.

"It's more rustic than I would have done but she's done a cute job. I love all the pictures... I recognize Roscoe, and I know Wynter has many pictures back in the North Pole of these same two boys. Is that Noah and his brother?"

"Yeah, man, they were young back then. I didn't know Wynter then. I guess she's changed a lot too."

"On the inside."

"But, not on the outside?"

"Not so much. We age slower than you."

"We age slower than the humans. How much slower do you age?"

"A lot slower. That's another similarity we share that makes me curious. We both age slower than the humans but the stronger the magic the slower the aging process."

"Huh, I hadn't thought about it before, but I guess you're right."

"Declan… are you going to tell your parents I'm back? I don't want you to fight again."

"I haven't talked to my parents since that night."

"Oh! Declan, please, don't do that. Go talk to them. You have to work things out with them. They're your parents. They're your family."

"I have nothing to say to them."

"Don't say that. You don't know how lucky you are. My mother didn't have any family left when she met my dad. She used to tell me stories all the time. She was so lonely until he found her."

"And, that's why family is so important to you, because your mother instilled it."

"Yes, and I'd rather leave and be miserable than make you miserable."

"I was miserable when you left."

"You have to talk to your parents."

"I'll do it not for them, for you." He placed a carefully gentle kiss on her sweet lips and said, "I'll go talk to them tonight, let you get settled, but tomorrow, it's just us. I'll show you around the South Pole."

"It's a deal," Star smiled.

Declan kissed her good bye and made her promise to be there when he got back in the morning then left for his parents.

Same as his last visit, Declan's mom met him excitedly at the door. "You're here!"

"I'm here," he said as he walked past her into the house.

His dad was standing just inside. "Son?"

"Star is back. She'll be sleeping inside a cave since she is clearly not welcome anywhere else."

"A cave?" Mom questioned.

"Yes."

"Where is she?" Dad asked.

She's not here if that's what you wanted to know, but she insisted that I come. It was her idea for me to come here tonight. If it were up to me, I wouldn't have come, but Star is big on family."

"Are you staying?" Mom asked.

"For a visit, yes."

"I didn't mean to…"

"What's done is done."

"You're serious about this girl."

It wasn't a question, so Declan didn't bother to respond. Instead he walked into the living room and sat down on the couch. He didn't know how long he was supposed to stay or what Star expected him to do now that he was here. He did know he was ready to leave, now. He didn't want to be any place where Star wasn't welcome.

"You're being childish, and you hurt your mother," Dad accused.

"I'm being childish? I'm not the one who judged a perfectly wonderful woman based solely on her last name. I bet if I had lied about her last name, you both would have loved Star. She's a beautiful person, inside and out. As miserable as her leaving made us both, she threatened to leave again tonight if I didn't come over here and make amends. She knew she wasn't welcome, but she wanted me to come.

"And, I'm sorry that Mom got her feelings hurt, but she wasn't the only one. When Star left that night, she didn't just leave your house. She left the South Pole

entirely. She left me, and it ripped me apart. I had no idea where she had gone. I didn't hear from her for a week. I wouldn't know where she was still if her brother hadn't come looking for me. I spent a week in agony. She was crying when I got to her. Her brother said that she had barely gotten out of bed in a week. So, I'm sorry that Mom got hurt, but tell her to join the club."

"You will not speak to your mother that way!"

"How about we not talk at all? I told Star I would come, and I have. I'm out of here."

"Please don't go," Mom begged baring the way out.

"Mom, I can't keep doing this. If you're going to make me choose between you and Star, I'm going to choose Star. I can't get her off my mind. I couldn't function when I thought she was gone for good. She's different. Everything just feels different with her. With other women I didn't care. I could take them or leave them. There were plenty more where that one came from, but there is only one Star Clause. They just don't make them like her. I can't… I can't lose her."

"I understand."

"So, you'll let me leave?"

"I wish you wouldn't… I was taken off guard last week… I'd like a second chance to get to know the girl my son loves."

Loves? He didn't say he loved her. Was that what all these feelings meant? Did he love her? Was that why it hurt so much when she left? Maybe he did love her.

"I don't know. I need to think about that."

"That's fine. Take your time."

Mom moved to the side and let Declan pass. Dad didn't say another word. That was probably for the best. Mom might have meant what she said about wanting a second chance, but that didn't mean that Dad did. Declan couldn't put Star back in the same situation a second time.

Chapter Six

Declan was bright and early the next day, and Star couldn't wait to get started. An entire day of just her, Declan, and the South Pole. Today was bound to be one of those wonderful days that would forever live on in her memory.

"Knock, knock," Declan called from the mouth of the cave.

"Come in."

"How did you sleep?" Declan asked coming over to kiss Star good morning.

"Like a baby. I told you this cave wouldn't be as rough as it sounded."

"I still worried about you out here all by yourself last night."

"Well, don't. I'm a big girl. I've been taking care of myself for a long time. I'll manage just fine until you get back. What's on the agenda today?"

"I thought we could start with breakfast. I'm starving."

Declan took Star to a small bakery. "They make the best biscuits in the South Pole. Just don't tell my mom I said that," he explained.

It smelled out of this world delicious. Star didn't doubt that they had delicious biscuits, but she wanted some of the amazing sugar cookies she could smell. Right up front behind a glass counter top sat a whole pan of hot, fresh sugar cookies. The aroma filled the tiny shop and made Star salivate.

Declan ordered a plate of bacon, eggs, and biscuits. Star ordered two sugar cookies and a plate of bacon. She was so excited about her bacon and cookies that it took her a moment to notice the odd look Declan was giving her.

"What? I told you I liked to eat bacon and sugar cookies together."

"Yeah, but... You weren't kidding."

"No, I wasn't," Star laughed.

"Must be a Clause thing."

Star cocked her head to the side and asked, "How so?"

"Don't the human kids leave cookies and milk for Santa on Christmas Eve?"

Star puzzled the idea for a moment before she laughed at the idea. "You know? I never thought to connect the two. My brother won't touch a cookie any other time of the year, because he gets more than his fill on Christmas Eve. Anthony on the other hand, he's training to take my brother's place this year. He must eat a dozen cookies a day, and I'm sure he'd eat more than that if Wynter would let him."

"I didn't know Anthony was taking over. What will your brother do?"

"Enjoy retirement mostly. I imagine he'll spend time spoiling that granddaughter."

¤ ¤ ¤ ¤ ¤

Declan couldn't keep from noticing the alarmed look on the face of the girl behind the counter when he said that Star's love of cookies must have been a Clause thing, and he didn't like it. He wanted to protect Star from every hurt. That girl was just lucky that Star didn't seem to notice.

Star chattered endlessly as they ate about this and that, about nothing really. It didn't matter what she talked about. As long as she was there with him and happy, nothing else mattered. Declan couldn't remember feeling that way about anyone. He had never hesitated in the past to hush up or tune out a jabbering woman who talked incessantly about nothing at all. Star was different though, and he found that he was actually listening.

She told him about the nuances of vampires, all the places she'd seen, what it was like traveling all the time, and when she ran out of stories, she asked him about his. He told her all about the sports he had played and the sports he taught or coached. He remembered antics and pranks he and his friends had pulled. He outlined what it was like to grow up an only child and what it was like going to school with other kids.

They spent hours sitting in the bakery talking, and Declan actually liked it. Sitting down and talking for hours at a time weren't something he would want to do every day, but with the right person every once in a while was... nice.

After they left the bakery, Declan took her by the
school first. There were kids outside playing on the
playground. Funny, Declan had never noticed before
the condition of the play equipment. Paint was faded
and chipping. Wood was splintering and splitting. Pieces
were coming lose. Honestly, it probably wasn't even safe
anymore.

Star pressed her hand against the window as
she leaned into it to get a better look. "Oh, don't they
look sweet?"

Slowly, subtly the play equipment reversed its aging
process. Declan watched Star carefully. She showed
no sign of what she was doing, but he knew she was
responsible for repairing the play equipment. She had
made her movements look natural. She didn't want him
to know what she had done, so Declan smiled and kept it
to himself. She was a thoughtful person and selfless.

Next he drove them to the heart of town and parked
the car so that they could get out and walk. As they
walked, he pointed out the different shops and described
the people who ran them. Most of the people wouldn't
react well to a Clause walking inside their establishment,
so Declan didn't make mention of going inside any of

them. He didn't want Star to have to go through that pain again.

They had walked up one side of the road and were about to cross the street and walk back down the other side when a passing car going too fast hit a pothole.

"Oh!" Star exclaimed.

The impact had to have rattled the driver's brain, and it most likely did damage to their car as well. "That's what they get. They shouldn't be going that fast downtown where pedestrians walk everywhere."

Declan didn't pay the car anymore attention as he pulled Star with him across the street. She held her hand flat discreetly by her side palm facing down as they walked past the pothole, and magically the pothole was filled in. She had done it again. She helped make repairs for a community that wouldn't help her if she were dying. She could put them in their place by making a big show of helping when they were hostile in return, but she didn't. She tried to cover what she had done to help each time. She wanted no recognition, no thanks.

A couple blocks later they came to a general store. The wooden sign that had always hung out above the sidewalk had come loose on one side. The wood was warped, and the paint was nearly gone completely.

Declan knew the older man who owned and ran the store had no business climbing up there to do repairs himself. His kids needed to get off their lazy tails and help him out around the store more, but they didn't.

Declan also knew that if he were to walk into that general store with a Clause on his arm, that old man wouldn't hesitate to point a rather large double barreled shotgun in their direction. He'd probably shoot too. That man had banned Noah from the store, because he said Noah was a Clause lover. Declan smiled to himself. If Noah, who was happily married to another South Poler, was a Clause lover, what would that make him who was dating a Clause or whatever it was he and Star were doing?

"That's a cute place," Star commented waving her fingers in the general direction of the general store like she was waving hello to the building itself.

Quietly the sign re-hung itself, the paint replenished itself, and the wood went back to its original shape. She had done it again, this time trying to make it look like she was merely gesturing to the general store.

"Why do you keep doing that?" Declan demanded.

"Doing what?" Star asked trying to play innocent, but turns out she was a lousy liar.

"Why do you keep fixing things for a community who hates you? Don't think they would do the same for you."

"What good is all this magic stuff if I can't help make the world a better place?" Star asked innocently. This time the innocence was genuine.

"You are a beautiful person, inside and out."

"That's what my daddy used to tell me," Star teased, but Declan was serious.

"Your daddy was a wise man."

"My daddy was a kind man but stubborn."

"I think I would have liked your daddy."

"Don't be so sure. He wouldn't have given a South Poler the time of day."

"The way my parents won't give you the time of day?" Declan turned it around.

The rest of the afternoon flew by as Declan showed off the South Pole and told her everything he could think of about the places they visited. As the sun set, Declan drove them up to look out point, and yes, it was exactly what it sounded like. It was a school night which meant lookout point would be deserted. Declan pulled up to the edge of the cliff and put the car in park.

"What is this place?" Star asked but didn't wait for an answer. She got up and walked to the Cliff side. Declan moved in behind her and wrapped his arms around her waist. "Wow, it looks so much like the North Pole."

"I hope you didn't have any place like this in the North Pole where there was only other family members," Declan snickered.

"Declan, you are a very naughty boy," Star scolded playfully.

"Guess, it's a good thing your brother doesn't pay any attention to us South Polers, or I'd be getting coal for Christmas."

"Be careful, the Clauses have been known to hold grudges."

"So have we." Declan nuzzled her neck and kissed her right behind the ear.

"Mmm, is this what we came up here for?"

"Yes," Declan answered as he continued to kiss her neck.

"In that case," Star replied as she turned around inside Declan's arms then she pressed her lips to his. They stayed at lookout point for some time holding each other, kissing each other, and enjoying the heat and passion that flowed too easily between them.

"Tomorrow, I thought maybe we could go to the courthouse and start looking up old records," Declan said as he walked Star back to… the cave.

"Thank you. I know that doesn't sound like much fun for you."

"Anything with you sounds like fun."

"You lie well," Star mused then kissed him good night.

Chapter Seven

Getting access to the records at the court house was easier said than done the next day. "She can't sign in here," the mousy looking receptionist said talking about Star rather than to her.

That alone was enough to make Declan's blood run hot, but it was what she did next that nearly set him off. She motioned for a security guard to come over. Perhaps Declan was more of a hot head than Noah gave him credit for. The only thing that kept Declan from going over the edge was that he knew this particular security guard. They had played on the same hockey team growing up. His name was Jeff Slate.

"Don't you lay a hand on her," Declan warned Jeff.

Jeff had the good sense to put both hands up in the air where Declan could see them. "What's the problem here?" he asked.

"This lady won't let us see public records," Declan said through clenched teeth.

"Louise?"

"This woman is a Clause. She shouldn't be in here in the first place, but she simply cannot sign out public records," Louise, the receptionist answered.

Jeff turned shocked eyes to Star and studied her like she was some side show freak. Declan was just getting ready to knock Jeff's teeth out when he moved his gaze to Declan. Finally a look of dawning came over Jeff's face, and he gave Declan an almost imperceptible nod. "Well, that may be, but Declan Anderson was born and raised right here. He's a natural citizen of the South Pole, and he has every right to sign out public records."

"He can, but she most assuredly cannot," Louise responded.

"Fair enough, right, De?"

"Sure," Declan agreed.

"I guess that's alright," Louise gave in reluctantly and turned a notebook around for Declan to sign in.

"There, no harm done," Jeff said as he clapped Declan on the shoulder. It was his unspoken way of telling Declan not to make him sorry he stood up for him. "Are any of the hockey teams looking promising this year?" he asked.

"There are some kids with raw talent if they'll focus."

"No one had the focus for sports like you. There will only be one De Anderson."

"Sure, thanks."

Declan took Star's hand and pulled her down the sterile hallway until they got to a door labeled public records.

"I like him... De?" Star snarked.

"It's just a nickname teammates give to each other. It's a camaraderie thing I guess."

"You make it sound like there is a special relationship between teammates."

"I guess so," Declan conceded as he threw himself down in a chair.

"Declan, are you ok?"

"She shouldn't have talked to you like that," Declan growled.

"It's ok," Star said sitting herself down in Declan's lap and snuggling against his chest. "I'm alright, and everything worked out just fine."

"Sure."

"You say that a lot," Star noted with a quirked smile. She kissed the side of his mouth and asked, "You better now?"

"Almost," Declan faked.

Star gave him a knowing smile and pressed her lips to his for a searing kiss.

"That's better."

"Good, because I've got some research to do."

Declan watched Star hop up and start rummaging through files. She hadn't been at it long when his phone started vibrating.

It was the ice rink. He had called to tell them he was taking the week off and would be out of reach. What were they doing calling him? He almost let it go to voicemail, but then he thought better of it at the last second and answered.

"Hello."

"I'm glad you answered the kids are all here for practice, and we've got a big problem," the head coach said.

"I told you I'm off this week."

"Yeah, I know, but this isn't about techniques. It's the ice. The ice is malfunctioning or something, and the maintenance guy is on some beach somewhere."

"I can't be there this week. Besides, I don't know what I could do." Declan sighed. "Fine, give me a few minutes. I'll be there."

He hung up and looked at Star who turned around and said, "We have to go, don't we?"

"Yeah, I'm sorry, but we'll come back. I promise."

The ice was a slushy mess when they got to the rink. "What happened?" Declan asked.

"I don't know. It's like it is melting or something. No one else is answering their phone," the head coach tried to explain.

"I don't know how to stop an indoor ice rink melting. Take practice outside. There's ice everywhere."

"It's cold out there," the coach fretted.

"Look, there are kids all over who cheerfully practice every day in the elements for love of the game. If your team can't practice out in the cold one day then they don't want it badly enough and my services are no longer needed."

Star waved her hand through the air palm facing the ice and then said, "It looks fine to me."

Sure enough, she had fixed the rink with magic.

"Wha-" the coach and players marveled.

"Thanks, Star," Declan said and gave her a big, sloppy kiss with all the boys whooping and hollering.

"No biggie," Star smiled.

The coach was watching her with wary eyes, but Declan knew beyond a shadow of doubt that he loved this beautiful woman with the even more beautiful heart.

By the time they got back to the court house it was only a couple hours before closing, and Star didn't make it through many of the file drawers before closing. They spend the next four days going through files.

"I don't get it," Star despaired. "There's no record of anything before the mid seventeen hundreds. It's like the South Pole wasn't even here."

"Maybe it wasn't. Maybe that's when our ancestors figured out we could survive the conditions and moved down here."

"But, why isn't there record of that? A date of colony establishment?"

"Maybe the first settlers didn't keep good records."

"I just don't buy that. There is something else going on here."

Declan pulled Star into his arms. "Is it really that important? Tonight is our last night in the South Pole tomorrow night we'll be going to the North Pole. I just want to spend the time together, enjoying each other's company. Can't we leave? We could go back to my place to get cleaned up and go out for dinner."

"Alright, but I still think that the lack of records are covering for something."

"That's fine. We can come back some time after Christmas. Deal?"

"Deal."

Chapter Eight

Star waited nervously for Declan to come out of the bathroom. He wasn't going to be happy about what she had done. There was no question about that. She did question, however, how he would react to her borrowing his phone.

At last the bathroom door opened. Steam and a smell that could only be described as pure male came wafting through the room. Was that aftershave? Was it a scent exclusively found in the South Pole, or did they have it imported in? Star stalled as she took a big whiff of that incredible smell that she would forever associate with Declan now.

He was dressed in dark jeans and a black button down. He was what she had always pictured in her mind as tall, dark, and handsome. He was unapologetically male, and he was every bit as protective as her brothers. He was funny. He didn't take himself too seriously but knew when a moment was serious. He was smart and a jock. He was everything she had ever looked for in a guy. She was quickly falling for him, and Star knew that if this thing between them went sour, she wouldn't survive it.

"What do you want to eat tonight?" he asked her.

"Home cooking?" Star asked optimistically.

"Home? You know I can't cook, right?"

"I know, but your mother can."

"My mother? No. It's not going to happen, Star. There's no way I'm putting you through that again."

"She's making pot roast, and I told her we'd be there by six."

"When did you even talk to my mom?"

"I borrowed your phone while you were in the shower."

"You what?"

"I borrowed your phone... Are you mad?"

Declan closed his eyes and gave his head a short vigorous shake like he was trying to wake up from a dream. "No, I'm not mad. I'm surprised."

He sat down on the bed and pulled Star into his lap. Star loved that he was always doing stuff like that, pulling her into his lap, holding her against his chest, holding her hand, or moving her hair behind her ear. She liked that he always wanted to be touching her.

"Why would you do that?" Declan asked.

"They're your family."

"I know that, and I know how important that is to you. But, I went and talked to them the other day just like you wanted. Didn't you believe me?"

"Of course, I believed you. I just wanted a second chance to get to know them. Unless you're uncomfortable with that." Declan tried to deny that it made him uncomfortable, but now that Star realized how quickly she was pushing him, she continued talking right over him. "Because, we don't have to go if you don't want to. I don't have to get along with your parents. They don't have to like me."

"Star, would you listen to me?"

"I know I was overstepping. We don't have to go."

"Star."

"It's ok. I shouldn't have called your parents like that."

The next thing Star knew she was flat on her back lying on the bed with Declan's lips crashing against her own. He was fast too. To get the drop on someone who fought vampires on a regular basis was impressive. Star sighed and relaxed as his lips moved over her own. This was bliss; she could lay here and kiss Declan forever.

Much, much later Declan pulled back and said, "Would you please listen to me now?"

Star couldn't remember what they had been talking about, but it couldn't be near as important as getting him to kiss her again. Her arms were still wrapped around his neck, so she pulled him back down to where she wanted him.

"Star." Declan disentangled Star's arms from around his neck and held them against the bed above her head. "I'm not mad. I don't want to see you hurt again, but I like that you want a second chance with my parents. I don't believe that it will work, but I love you for trying."

¤ ¤ ¤ ¤ ¤

Did he just say that? He did. He told Star he loved her, and she didn't even flinch. It was the truth, but it was too early to tell her that. They had only known each other for eight months. Out of those eight months they had been around each other less than two weeks. It was way too soon to tell her he loved her whether it was true or not. He was going to scare her off.

Star gave an experimental tug on her wrists, but Declan was holding her too securely for her to escape. "We don't have to go anywhere," Star moaned as she pulled herself up trying to reach his lips again.

Far be it for Declan to deny a person that sweet what they want most, so he did the gentlemanly thing and kissed her again… and again… and again. When he finally came up for air, it was six o'clock.

"Star, we need to leave. You told my mom we'd be there by six."

"Are we going?" Star asked clearly confused.

"Yes, we can go, but the moment they cross the line, we're out of there."

"Yea, we'll get along. I'll make sure of it."

"I don't know about that. My dad can't stand tardiness."

"I can't make another bad impression," Star worried just before she transported them magically to his parents' living room.

"Man, that's disorienting but convenient. Warn me next time."

"Sorry." Then she added more to his parents, "I just didn't want us to be late."

Declan rolled his eyes and explained, "It was my fault we lost track of time."

"Yes, we can see that," Dad said trying and failing not to crack a smile.

Star gave Declan a confused look. Her eyes grew wide with surprise, and she waved her hand in front of his mouth. Seeing the smeared lipstick around Star's lips, he figured he was wearing his own share of smeared lipstick. He smiled as he wiped at the worst of the smears covering Star. "You've got a little something there yourself."

"Oh." Star turned her back to everyone in the room and sort of ducked down to be sure no one else could see as she waved her hand in front of her own face. "Is that better she asked turning back to Declan.

"It's perfect, not that I found the first way all that objectionable."

Star gave Declan's arm a playful slap and said, "Stop."

Mom burst out laughing, and Declan wondered what in the world had happened now.

"Oh me!" Mom exclaimed. "I wish I'd had magic like that back when I was dating Ralph. I got in so much trouble coming home with smeared lipstick that I quit wearing the stuff all together."

Then Declan started to laugh too, because it was kind of funny thinking about his parents getting in trouble for making out. Eventually Dad joined in the laughter as well, and only Star stood there looking perplexed.

"I guess it was sort of wasted on a girl with only brothers around… We did leave home at eighteen, but for the first few years all your focus is on staying alive. Boys are not a primary concern," Star mused mostly to herself.

"Oh, you were sheltered," Mom tried to sober. "There weren't any other kids around?"

"Oh, no ma'am, as far as I know no one but Clauses have ever lived in the North Pole. We never even see people outside our own family until we leave to take our place fighting vampires. Well, everyone but the eldest male, he stays to take over the role of Santa. Personally, I feel sorry for my brother. While the rest of us went out to make a life of our own, he stayed home for years just waiting for Daddy to retire… But, you didn't want to know any of that, because you hate the Clauses… I'm sorry. It's just so nice not having to hide my magic for a change that I forget. I forget that… Well, I forget that you hate me."

"Oh, nonsense. Declan loves you, and we'll learn to love you too. Isn't' that right, Ralph?"

"Yeah, yeah."

It was obvious that Mom had a little talk with Dad prior to tonight. Either way, Declan was glad he was listening.

"The food's on the table," Mom said shooing Declan and Dad toward the dining room. Then she took Star by the arm and said, "Come on. You can tell me more about how you hide so much magic."

Star gave his mom a genuine smile, and Declan was thankful that his mom was making a real effort to get along. He only wished she'd quit telling Star he loved her before Star got scared off.

Mom and Star chatted throughout the meal, about this and that but mostly about boys they had dated. That irked Declan. He didn't want to think about his mom dating anyone besides Dad, but he especially did not want to think about Star dating anyone but him. By the end of the meal he felt like he was nothing but a writhing mass of jealousy. He was tense and irritable. He felt like he was being challenged. He was bowed up ready to meet the challenge head on, except there was no one there to fight.

"How long are you staying?" Dad asked Star.

"We leave tomorrow."

"We?" Mom asked Declan.

"Yeah, a week here, a week there. We're going to the North Pole tomorrow."

"The North Pole!" Dad reacted. Uh oh, that might have just pushed Dad over his limit.

"Yeah, my brother is busy training..." Star looked at Mom and cut off what she was about to say. "Anyway, everyone's busy, but I wanted to check out some of the history records in the attic."

"Star is curious what started the feud between the North and South Poles," Declan explained.

"Oh, is it safe?" Mom asked.

Declan rolled his eyes. "It's her family home. I guess she's safe enough."

"I meant is it safe for you?"

"I've been there once before and came back safe and sound; unless, you're trying to pretend that never happened."

"I promise he'll be perfectly safe, Mrs. Anderson. Even if my family were a danger, which I give you my word they're not, they're so busy this time of year, they'll hardly notice us there. I wouldn't be at all surprised if we don't see them the whole time we're there."

Dad grumbled something about a Clause's word, but Mom deliberately spoke over him. "You will be careful, won't you?"

"Yes, Mom, but really what do you think will happen? Do you think the jolly man delivering toys to children around the world will kill us in our sleep?"

Star laughed out loud at that one. "Santa wouldn't know if a real fight came knocking on his door. Come to think of it, a real fight did come knocking on his door in March, didn't it... Noah was protecting him. Oh, Noah tried not to make it too obvious, but I don't think

Santa ever raised a finger. Now, vampires? They really would kill you in your sleep and never think twice about it. I know you met Anthony, but he really wasn't a true picture of what a vampire is. He was very different from the very beginning."

"How long have you known Anthony?" Mom asked.

"I didn't actually meet him until the wedding, but I've heard Wynter talk about him until I feel like I've always known him. My sister, Mary, met him the night he was turned; although, that wasn't a very pleasant meeting. He was-"

Declan placed a hand over Star's when Mom started to look sick.

"I'm sorry. My family always says I talk too much, and Anthony's fine now. Really. He's happy."

"Well, I'm glad to hear that. I always did like that boy, and I like talking with you," Mom said, and Declan wanted to hug her.

"Thank you. I like talking to you too, and I hope we get to do it again."

"Soon," Mom added.

"We should get going," Declan said. He had shared Star's attention long enough, and he wanted her all to himself.

Chapter Nine

Star and Declan left for the North Pole the next day shortly after lunch. It didn't take nearly as long as Declan's first trip to the North Pole, and it was a lot cheaper since they didn't need airfare. It didn't even take as long as his first trip back home in the sled. It took no time at all. Star used magic the same way North had, but when Declan came up with North, he was too worried about Star to take notice of anything else.

Star had not been kidding about her family being busy either. The house was completely deserted when they arrived. Declan followed Star upstairs. As they passed the second door on the right, Declan asked, "Isn't that your room?"

"Yes, I was going to show you your room. The closest room to mine is Wynter's old room and Mary's before that, but it is still decorated rather girly. I think you'd be more comfortable in one of the boys' old rooms."

She walked all the way to the opposite end of the hall. Then she turned and led Declan into a room with light blue walls. The furniture was natural wood, and the bed covers and curtains were dark brown. The walls were covered in posters of classic cars.

"This was Israel's room."

"Wow, he must have really liked cars."

"Not really," Star said with a sad shake of her head. She unpinned one of the posters, and it fell away to reveal a scantily clad girl in a bikini. "Israel liked girls. Mama never found the posters, but there's a different girl under every poster. I don't think he ever told his wife about them either. You wouldn't know it to look at him today, but once upon a time, Israel was the rebellious middle child. He used to give my parents fits, but I thought he hung the moon… Before I knew better, I wanted to be just like the girls that Israel had hiding in his room. It wasn't too hard with magic to duplicate the bikinis. Oh, but when my mother caught me parading around the house in one, you would have thought I killed someone."

Declan looked back at the pinup. It was some bleach blonde in a barely there leather bikini much like the black leather Star had worn when they fought side by side. He looked back at Star with a mischievous grin and said, "I wouldn't mind seeing you in something like that."

Star tried to hide her smile. "Yes, well, there will be no more of that," she scolded as she secured the corvette back over the pinup.

Declan stepped up and wrapped Star up tightly against his chest. "Why'd you bring me to this room then?" he whispered into her ear.

"It has the best view." She pulled him over to look out a tiny window at the side of a mighty snow covered mountain. "But, I better not catch you in here ogling those posters."

"I wouldn't dream of it. I'll be ogling you instead. I can't promise I won't be dreaming of you in a leather bikini though."

"Tease! You want to know the ironic part though? The girl Israel married is a real good girl, two steps short of prude, but Mary tells me all the time that it's a good thing Mother isn't here to see the way I dress."

"Absolutely scandalous," Declan said slowly running his hands down her side to her hips. He pulled her as close as he could get her and kissed her.

The next morning Declan woke to the feel of Star's warm, soft lips pressed to his temple, then the corner of his mouth, and his first coherent thought was that he must have died and gone to heaven.

"Wake up, sleepy head. Time for breakfast."

Declan pushed himself to a sitting position, and Star sat a tray of eggs and bacon in front of him and two sugar cookies. "I hope you didn't cook this."

Star tried not to smile. "Don't be mean. My sister in law left if for us."

He leaned over to kiss her good morning and was met with the fresh taste of mint. "You've already brushed your teeth?"

"I've been up for a couple hours. I wanted to bring you breakfast and let you know where I would be before I headed to the attic."

"Wait, and I'll go with you."

"I'm a big girl," she reminded him.

"Is it wrong that I want to spend all my time with you?"

"I hope not."

Declan stole another kiss before he started stuffing eggs in his mouth.

Twenty minutes later they were in the attic going through dusty old boxes. "This looks promising," Declan said picking up a box full of letters.

Star opened the first one and smiled. "It's a letter to Santa. It's dated before Daddy's time. It must have been during grandfather's time as Santa, but why would we keep these old letters? He would have gotten thousands more than this in only one year."

"Read it and see."

Star smiled and began reading out loud. "Dear Santa, my friends say that it is foolish to believe in Santa at eighteen, but I care not. I do believe in you. More so, I believe you are a good man. What you do for boys and girls all over the world is both kind and selfless. You must put so much time and effort into your work. What thanks do you get? People stop believing in you. That is the thanks you get, yet I am writing this letter to thank you for all that you do. Thank you, Santa. Love, Rose." Star stopped and gave the letter a curious look.

"What is it?"

"My grandmother's name was Rose."

"Read the next one. Maybe there's a connection."

"Dear Santa, you must get many letters each year. I suppose you cannot remember them all. I wrote to you last year. I did not request toys. I am much too old for such things. Rather, I wrote to thank you from a world of adults who have forgotten all you do for a world most ungrateful.

"I wish that I could say I am writing again this year with only thanks in my heart, but I am afraid that I find myself dreadfully lonely. Nineteen is terribly old to be unwed, and mother and father both died from dysentery earlier this year. If it is not too much trouble, what I would like most is a little company. Love Rose."

Declan had the next letter opened and ready. He handed it to Star, who kept reading.

"Dear Rose. This one is from grandfather! He actually wrote her back! Imagine that!"

"What's it say?"

"Dear Rose, of course I remember your letter of thanks. It was the first of its kind that I have ever received. I saved the letter for sentimental purposes.

"I do not believe that nineteen is too old to be unwed. I am considerably older than that and as of yet unwed. I was sorry to hear about your parents. Mine too are departed. It saddens me more to know you are lonely. I am sorry to reply there is nothing I can do to provide company. Sincerely, Santa."

"Do you think Rose was your Grandmother Rose?"

"She must have been. Santa doesn't write return letters. There are just too many to answer them all."

"Here," Declan said, and that was the last time he interrupted.

> Dear Santa,
>
> I was thrilled to receive your letter! It could have proven to my friends once and for all that you are real, Yet I did not show the letter to a soul. I have kept it though.
>
> You must think me a silly little girl to complain so. You must be ever so much lonelier than I. Do you have anyone at all where you come from? Do you truly live at the North Pole?
>
> Love,
>
> Rose

Dear Rose,

Yes, I truly live at the North Pole, and no, there is no one else here excepting for the elves and reindeer. There are magical wards that prevent others from finding my workshop. I stay busy, but it is lonely at times. I have brothers and sisters that pay me a visit from time to time. Also, I look forward to your correspondence.

Yours truly,
Santa

Dear Santa,

I am so sorry that you are alone, yet I was honored that you look forward to my letters. It is rewarding to think that I can bring you a small portion of the joy that your letters have brought me.

This has been a brighter year. I am still unwed, but I accept that about myself. I have also taken the job as the new school teacher after the last one passed suddenly. I can offer only a temporary replacement while one more qualified is found. I am glad though for something to fill my days.

Love,

Rose

Dear Rose,

Your letters bring me great joy. They are the highlight of my year, and I am glad to hear that your year has been a better one.

I told my brother about you on his latest visit. He thinks I am smitten, and I think that he might be correct. He thinks me a fool to not meet you in person, but then I know my brother to be impulsive.

Love,

Santa

Dear Santa,

It would be a most atrocious lie if I said I was not smitten with you as well. I know that it is perfectly scandalous for me to admit such, more so to admit that I do long to meet you face to face. But then that is horrendous for me to say. Please forget I said it.

I am still teaching as they have not yet found a replacement. The lessons are getting harder as the children get older, but I have grown fond of them.

Love,

Rose

Dear Rose,

I cannot forget that you want to meet face to face, because I want that as well. Alas, there is no future for us. You are needed where you are to teach the children, and I am needed where I am. I could never leave my job at the North Pole without heir, nor could I ask you to live here where it is so cold.

Love,

Santa

Dear Santa,

A more educated teacher has taken the position at the school, and I could not be happier for the students. Also it is terribly hot here. I was contemplating moving somewhere cooler. Do you know where I would find such a place?

I still wish for us to meet. If you are not horrified by my boldness, I will try to wait up for you this Christmas Eve. If you do not show, then I will know your answer.

Love,

Rose

Dear Rose,

I miss you terribly, my love, and I anxiously await the day that I will bring you home to the North Pole. I talked with my brother, and he has agreed to meet us here when we return this Christmas Eve. We will be married on Christmas Day.

Love always,

Santa

"Awe, that is the sweetest thing," Star gushed. "Grandma Rose told me once that she and Grandfather were married on Christmas Day, but she never told me the whole story."

"Look at the date," Declan urged her gently.

The last letter was dated 1854.

"That long ago their story was one of scandal, not the sort of thing you told your grandkids," Declan described.

"Still, I think a Clause wedding on Christmas Day would be incredibly romantic," Star admitted.

"Maybe someday you'll get your Christmas wedding." And, maybe I'll be the one to give it to you, Declan thought. The thought took him by surprise. Things were moving way too fast. He had never felt this way about anyone, and he wasn't sure what to do about it.

Chapter Ten

Star was excited the next day to go back to the attic. Finding Grandfather and Grandma Rose's letters had been wonderful. Declan could be right about them being ashamed of their story, but Star thought it was a love story for the ages.

There was no telling what they would find today. After yesterday, anything was possible. Stepping into the attic to explore was a fabulous adventure. Star was practically bouncing on the balls of her feet with anticipation. She was so ready to get started.

"Slow down, Star. The stuff's not going anywhere," Declan teased.

"Hurry up!"

Declan gave Star a smile that she had come to associate with him being up to something. He grabbed her arm and gave a quick tug sending her tumbling into him. He caught her against his chest and held her fast as he lowered his head to hers for a kiss.

Star waited for the kiss to end, because really Declan was an amazing kisser. She didn't want to miss a single kiss, but when the kiss ended, she slapped his chest and accused, "You're wasting time."

"Kissing you is never a waste of time," the smooth talker rattled off. Star was somewhat sure that other girls had heard that same line many times from his lips, but she couldn't help but smile anyway.

She took Declan's hand and practically ran up the attic stairs.

They spent hours going through boxes of old toys. You would think that with a workshop full of elves so close that toys wouldn't be such a keepsake, but it appeared that every generation had kept toys their children played with. Star even found a box of her own dolls.

Declan pulled a sheet off of some old piece of furniture that turned out not to be furniture at all. It was a large framed painting of... well, it was the spitting image of Joseph as a young man, but Star knew full well that Joseph had never posed for a painting in his life. No way would anyone ever convince Joseph that it was worth standing still that long.

"Did Joseph get a big enough portrait of himself?" Declan asked.

"That's not Joseph."

"What are you talking about? It looks just like him."

"I know, but he's never had a painting done of himself."

"Um, Star, this painting says differently."

"I know what it looks like, but I would know if he had this done. Help me lift it up and look behind it."

Declan moved the painting forward and leaned it against himself like it weighed little to nothing even though Star knew that not to be true. She squeezed behind between the painting and the wall and found a square of paper with a name and date taped to the back of the painting.

"Declan! You won't believe this! This is a painting of my great-great-grandfather."

"You're kidding. He looks just like Joseph."

"Mother always said if there were any of us who couldn't deny the Clause blood it was Joseph."

Declan carefully placed the painting back against the wall. "That's wild. Do you think he's ever seen it?"

"I'm sure he hasn't."

"You should tell him it's up here. He might want to check it out."

The painting was the only thing of real interest that they found that day, but Star counted it a good day nevertheless. The painting was so interesting.

The next day Star found a box of old photographs, very old photographs. They were the kind that took so long that no one actually smiled in them, and there was a box full right in front of Star. She started going through the photographs and seeing Joseph's face, she knew right away that these were photographs of her great-great-grandfather. There were ones of him and his siblings and parents. Star was struck by how much her daddy had resembled her great-great-great-grandfather. There were also later pictures of her great-great-grandfather with his wife and children. Star wondered which one of the boys had been her great-grandfather and if she would ever know.

"I found a box of photos of my great-great-grandfather and his family," Star told Declan.

"Yeah? I found three boxes of photos of you and your brothers and sisters growing up."

"Really? I always wondered what Mother did with all the old photos."

They ended up taking the four boxes of pictures down to Star's room where they spent the rest of the day looking at pictures together and laughing.

On their fourth day in the North Pole Declan dug all the way to the back of the attic where he found a box full of books. At least he thought they were books until he opened the first one and found a handwritten entry.

"Star, I think I found some dude's diary."

"I think it's proper to call it a journal," Star giggled.

"Whatever," Declan said with a roll of his eyes. A guy keeping a journal still sounded a little pansy to him. "Did you want to take a look?"

"Yeah, is there a name on them? Star asked as she made her way over to Declan.

"Sinister, no wait, Sinter Klaussen. It might not be from your family at all."

"Yes it is! That was my great-great-great-grandfather's name!"

"How did it get changed from Sinter Klaussen to Santa Clause?"

"Who knows how these things happen. Oh, there are a lot of them."

"Yeah, and they're heavy."

"Do you think we could get them downstairs?"

"No problem."

"I could use magic if they're too heavy," Star suggested.

"Star, never tell a man something is too heavy for him to carry. Then it becomes a challenge."

"Please don't hurt yourself," Star laughed.

"Lead the way, beautiful," and he hoisted up the big box.

The journals were not in order, and it took all day to get them in order. It probably would have gone faster if Declan hadn't insisted on taking so many breaks for kissing, not that Star was ever heard complaining.

¤ ¤ ¤ ¤ ¤

Star was already sitting cross legged in the middle of her bed reading the journals when Declan got up the next morning.

"You haven't been up all night have you?"

"Nah, I got up with the sun. I just couldn't wait to get started. This is really interesting. He started keeping journals from the very beginning. He talked about how they came to the North Pole and how they got started. It was more than just our family too! There were two families that started the legend of Santa Clause, Sinter Klaussen and Christopher Nikolajsen. I don't know yet what happened to Christopher Nikolajsen and his family, but they certainly haven't been a part of the operation for some time."

Declan sat down behind Star and kissed her bare neck as he started reading over her shoulder. The two men must have been close the way this Sinter guy raved about Christopher. "Sounds like they were friends."

"Best friends, that's why they decided to start the business together," Star corrected.

They had been reading for hours, one boring entry after another. Declan was just about sure he could run the North Pole himself by this point, but Star was still riveted to every word. He didn't know how Star did it,

Declan's eyes were tired and the words beginning to blur together.

"How about I go make us some sandwiches?" Declan suggested, thinking he could use a break even if Star didn't.

Declan took his time making the sandwiches. He didn't necessarily want to get back to those stupid journals. If that wasn't where Star was, he probably would have found himself something else to do.

The house was still so quiet. Declan had an idea how much work went into this whole Christmas Eve thing in the beginning, and today it must have all been run on a much grander scale. It was no wonder everyone was so busy. It was meant to be run by two families when it was started. That was a lot of work for only one family.

When Declan got back upstairs with lunch, Star was crying. He rushed to her side. "Star? What happened?"

"Christopher's youngest daughter doesn't want to hunt vampires. It's just like Mary."

"Mary didn't want to be a vampire hunter? She's so tough."

"She is now, but that's because the life of a hunter has hardened her. She detested the idea. She didn't want to be a hunter, but she was forced to follow family tradition. My great-great-great-grandfather is insisting Christopher's daughter do it the same way Daddy insisted Mary do it. It's dreadful, and it's causing a horrible fight between the two families."

"Star, what's done is done. This, these journals, they're all in the past," Declan tried to sooth as he removed hair from Star's face and wiped away her tears.

"I know, but they are just fighting so much. There's so much hate building. I think this might be what split the two families."

"Why don't you stop reading for a while and eat?"

"I can't. I have to know what happened."

Declan didn't think this was very healthy, but it was obvious that Star had no intentions of backing down. Instead Declan pulled Star into his lap and held her as she continued to read.

"Oh no! Declan listen to this," Star said, and she began to read aloud. "Christopher still refuses to press Amity to join the hunt. He declared today that he will take his family and relocate to the South Pole to start again. I reminded him that his magic was God given and that if he did not use it as He intended then the magic would surely fade. Christopher did not care… Declan, what was Noah's last name?"

"Nikola, you know, like that inventor."

"Nikola, like Nikolajsen, like Christopher Nikolajsen."

"You don't think…"

"I do… That's what started the feud between the North and South Poles. Two best friends, one blinded by his sense of duty, one blinded by love for his family, both too stubborn to meet in the middle."

Star turned and buried her head against his chest. She was crying again. Declan wanted to burn those journals for all the pain they were causing his Star. His Star? When had he begun to think of her as his?

Declan shook off the wayward thought and petted Star's back. "Hey, hey, this is a good thing. We can tell everyone what really happened and call this feud off. Any South Polers who want to join the hunt can do so. Any Clauses who want to retire to the South Pole can. Maybe we can even get your brother and Anthony some help up here. I'd say they're running their selves ragged up here."

"Maybe you're right… It will only disrupt things at first, and this is their busiest time of the year. Couldn't we wait until after the new year to tell anyone?"

"Sure, if that's what you want."

"I want to get out of here."

"Alright, where do you want to go?"

No sooner had Declan asked the question, he was sitting on the couch in his parents' living room with Star still in his lap.

"Oh, mercy!" Mom screamed in terror.

Dad was out of his chair in a heartbeat roaring like a great polar bear.

"It's just us," Declan assured them.

"Don't do that!" Dad barked. "I could have killed you both."

"Star, whatever is the matter?" Mom asked.

"It was so terrible," Star said thrusting the offending journal into Mom's lap. So much for not telling anyone.

Mom read the journal and reread it. "There, there, child, everything is going to be alright." Never mind that Star was technically older than Declan's mom, the woman was still trying to calm Star as if the girl were one of her own kids.

Declan looked at his dad who motioned him into the kitchen. Declan looked back at Star sobbing at Mom's knee and reluctantly followed Dad into the kitchen.

"It's best to let your mom handle this, woman to woman," Dad advised. "What was in that blasted book?"

"It's the journal of Sinter Klaussen, Star's great-great-great-grandfather. He started that whole Christmas Eve thing with a man named Christopher Nikolajsen. When Nikolajsen's daughter didn't want to become a vampire hunter it started a feud between the two families, and Nikolajsen decided to move his family to the South Pole even though Klaussen warned it would weaken their magic. Star believes that Noah's family shortened the name to Nikola at some time and that we are all descended from Nikolajsen."

"I can't say that I disagree," Dad said in a stunned voice. "It would explain a lot."

"I didn't think Star was going to tell anyone. She said this was the busiest time of year for her family and that it would be best to wait until after the new year. She brought us here though, and-" Declan spread his arm

out toward the living room where they had left Star
and Mom.

"That girl's parents are both gone, aren't they?"

"How did you know?"

"One of the things you'll learn about women, son, is
that at a time like this they want to be with their mothers
to have them tell them everything is going to be ok.
When you can't be with your own mother, a mother in
law is the next best thing."

"A mother in law?"

"That's right."

"Dad?"

Dad didn't say anything. He just waited for Declan to
find the words he was looking for.

"Do you think Star and I could be married?"

"I don't see why not. Things won't be easy, but the
best things in life seldom are."

Chapter Eleven

Declan's mom insisted that Star stay with them tonight. She said that alone in a cave somewhere was no place to be when you were distraught. It was very kind of her, and Star would forever be grateful. Even if the Anderson's didn't like her yet, Mrs. Anderson had shown Star great compassion this afternoon.

Declan also refused to leave his parents' house. He said that Star was upset and he needed to be close. Of course the cad had offered to stay in the same room to keep an eye on her, but his old bedroom was next door to the guest room. Star told him that was close enough and that she would call out if she needed him.

Star loved him so much. She didn't know what she would do when Christmas was over and it was time for her to go back to vampire hunting. It wasn't that she

minded the hunt. It was sort of fun. It kept you on your toes, but she couldn't imagine leaving Declan now. He was a part of her life. He was a part of her. Somewhere along the way, she had given him a piece of her heart, and it would rip her apart to leave him now.

All night long Star tossed and turned thinking about Declan and how hard it was going to be to leave. Then in the early morning hours the door creaked and slowly started to creep open.

"Star? Are you awake?"

"Yes."

The door swung open all the way as Declan let himself in. He shut the door behind him and said, "We need to talk."

Star didn't say anything as Declan moved to the bed. He sat down on the edge and looked down at his lap.

"I know we haven't known each other all that long, but I don't want you to leave."

"I don't want to leave either," Star agreed.

"I know you're a vampire hunter and all."

"I could give it up," Star quickly decreed.

"You want a Christmas wedding, and I was just thinking that next year would be a long time to wait."

"I don't want to wait."

"You don't?" Declan looked up as if hearing her for the first time.

"No, I don't."

"So, you'll marry me?"

"Yes!" Star threw herself at Declan and wrapped her arms around his neck.

He let out a relieved sigh and said, "I don't have a ring."

"Let me!" Star gasped. She knew just the ring she wanted for her Christmas wedding. She held out her hand and gazed as the perfect engagement ring appeared. It was a gold band that crisscrossed back and forth on the top half and diamonds and rubies were embedded alternating in the crisscrossed part of the band. Sitting on top was the largest diamond of them all. It seemed to scream out the joyous news, the announcement of a new life together.

Although she didn't know how Declan's parents would react, Star couldn't wait to show Mrs. Anderson the minute she woke up.

"Look!" she cried thrusting her left hand in front of Mrs. Anderson.

"When did that happen?"

"Only two hours ago," Star replied.

"An unconventional start for an unconventional couple," Mr. Anderson mumbled. "I can't deal with this, this early in the morning. I need coffee." Then they moved on to the kitchen.

"Congratulations," Mrs. Anderson offered. "I'm glad I was wrong about you, Star. Do you have a date in mind?"

"We want to get married on Christmas Day!"

"Christmas Day? That is soon. Could I suggest a destination wedding? Something far from the South Pole?"

Declan burst out laughing. "We were thinking of something quiet. The South Pole isn't ready for us, and Star will tell her family after the new year. Maybe just us and you and dad?"

"As long as I'm invited that sounds just wonderful."

"Of course you're invited," Star supplemented. "A Christmas wedding will be perfect! Don't you think?"

"I think it will," Mom agreed.

¤ ¤ ¤ ¤ ¤

Christmas Day was perfect. Declan and his dad were dressed in tuxes with a red vest and tie. Mrs. Anderson was in a red floor length dress that flared out at the hips. It had delicate, beaded embroidery, and the sleeves and bodice were fur lined. Star's dress was best of all. It was strapless and form fitted down to mid thigh where it flared the tiniest bit. Over it she wore a white hooded cape that was fur lined and flared out all around her to form a train. Her midnight hair was down in loose curls, and she carried a bouquet of red roses.

The minister was the only other attendant, but that didn't matter. A large wedding or small, Star was marrying the man of her dreams. Afterwards they celebrated with a decadent white cake that was four layers tall and had red and white snowflakes cascading down one side. Everything was absolutely perfect as far as Star was concerned, and Declan couldn't wipe the smile off his face.

That night Star had a special surprise for Declan.

¤ ¤ ¤ ¤ ¤

After the wedding, Declan and Star went back to his place, their place. He couldn't believe he had really gone through with it. She was Mrs. Star Anderson.

Speaking of, was she coming out of that bathroom anytime soon, or was she planning to hide in there all night, on their wedding night of all nights?

"Star, what are you doing in there?"

"I'm ready," she called. "Close your eyes."

"Seriously?"

"Just do it."

Declan rolled his eyes then closed them. He would do anything for Star. "Ok, they're closed. Now will you tell me what you're doing?"

"Open your eyes."

She was closer now. Her voice was no longer muffled by the bathroom door. Declan opened his eyes and forgot to breathe. Star was standing in the middle of the room dressed only in what amounted to little more than a string bikini. It was cherry red, or maybe it was meant to be Christmas red and fur lined. Strangely there were bells hanging from the strings hugging her hips. On her head she wore the classic Santa Clause hat and her beautiful raven hair hung down around her shoulders. Star looked like Mrs. Clause had just made the cover of Playboy, and she was all his, his Christmas Star.

"Do you like it?" she asked. "I got the idea from one of Israel's swimsuit models. The bells were my touch just like the ones on Santa's sleigh. What do you think?"

"I think you better get over here."

<h1 style="text-align:center">Epilouge</h1>

There was still a long way to go in reuniting the North and South Poles. Star's family couldn't have been happier for her and Declan, and the South Polers… Well, they'd get used to the union eventually.

Star gave up hunting vampires and settled down in the South Pole with Declan. He was still protective as ever and quick to fight if someone was mean to Star, but some things never change.

Star started her own line of clothing. People were resistant at first simply because she was a Clause, but in the end they gave in. She carried men's, women's, and children's clothes. She had everything from casual wear to formal wear, even lingerie, and her sense of style and quality couldn't be beat.

Declan continued his sports instruction and eventually opened his own hockey rink where he gave personalized lessons.

Kids? Kids were most definitely a part of the equation, but that is a story for another time.

Also Available From Elizabeth Lee Sorrell

Wrong Turn Fairy Tales

Gwynn worked hard to live up to her family's expectations putting away all childish things and even a few childhood friends. Now she is about to marry Addison, a very sensible, very rich businessman, but before she can say yes to his proposal, she finds herself falling through one fairy tale after another. Will she find her happily ever after with her very own prince charming, or has her fairy tale taken a wrong turn?

Exclusively found from Barnes & Nobles for Nook Book.

More Than Instinct

Kat had a past best left forgotten. Jackson had a past he couldn't get over, but when circumstances throw them together in a dangerous game, they had to find a way to work together. What they would find was that, "This whole mess had bonded them in a way that could never be undone."

Available from your favorite bookstore in paperback and ebook.

Black & White

Shantelle White has been with a top secret branch of the CIA from its very beginning. Jayson Black is one of the branches top operatives. When funds get tight Shantelle and Jayson are forced together to find a solution. Will they find out where the money has gone and who is behind it before all their agents are gone?

Available from your favorite bookstore in paperback and ebook.